Don't miss the other stories in the
Lollapalooza short story series:

Quarantine
Common Enemies
Coiled Danger
Mars Meeting

R.W. WALLACE
AUTHOR OF THE VANGUARD

QUARANTINE

A LOLLAPALOOZA SHORT STORY

BOOK 1

Quarantine

by R.W. Wallace

Copyright © 2019 by R.W. Wallace

Copy editing by Jinxie Gervasio

Cover by the author

Cover Illustration 47588248 © algolonline | 123rf.com

All characters and events in this book, other than those clearly in the public domain, are fictitious and any resemblance to real persons, living or dead, is purely coincidental.

All rights reserved. No part of this publication may be reproduced, distributed, or transmitted in any form or by any means, including photocopying, recording, or other electronic or mechanical methods, without the prior written permission of the publisher, except in the case of brief quotations embodied in critical reviews and certain other noncommercial uses permitted by copyright law.

www.rwwallace.com

ISBN: [979-10-95707-23-3]

Main category—Fiction

Other category—Science Fiction

First Edition

Also by R.W. Wallace

Mystery

THE TOLOSA MYSTERY SERIES
The Red Brick Haze (free)
The Red Brick Cellars
The Red Brick Basilica

GHOST DETECTIVE SHORTS (COMING SOON)
Just Desserts
Lost Friends
Family Bonds
Till Death
Common Ground

SHORT STORIES
Hidden Horrors
Cold Blue Eternity
Critters
Gertrude and the Trojan Horse
First Impressions
Let Them Eat Cake
Two's Company

Science Fiction (short stories)
The Vanguard

Adventure (short stories)
Size Matters

Fantasy (short stories)
Morbier Impossible
A Second Chance
Unexpected Consequences

QUARANTINE

Captain Kovak kept her eyes on the controls as her ship eased into the docking station. Buttons lit up, then shut back down as their function was fulfilled. Warning beeps sounded as one side of the ship got too close to the surrounding walls, then shut off as the automatic pilot adjusted the trajectory. Information scrolled past on the main surveillance screen, informing the reader of every engine thrust, every rudder position, every danger detected. The captain read them all, not letting her guard down simply because they were no longer in outer space.

The cockpit was eerily silent, with only the clangs from clamps grabbing the Lollapalooza's docking fixtures ringing through the hull at regular intervals. They were up to eleven—Captain Arleen Kovak kept count—with only five to go. The last couple of feet should not present any danger to ship or crew.

Arleen glanced over at her copilot, Yosu Gaal. Handsome as sin, but after eight months on the same ship, still a stranger.

He also kept his attention on the ship's log, deep-set green eyes missing nothing. He sat ramrod straight in his chair, harness still in place even though there was no danger of the Lollapalooza crashing.

Arleen liked that about him. He hadn't necessarily been one to always keep his harness on while traveling, but he'd understood it was important to her, and he respected her wishes.

Or her OCD, as the late Captain Maric would have said.

Arleen never heard Yosu say anything pejorative about her as a person, nor of her way of running the ship. The problem was, she never heard him say anything positive, either. He just went along with everything, a slight smile playing along his luscious lips, and chewing his ever-present chewing gum.

She'd never seen him actually put one in his mouth. She was starting to wonder if it was possible to chew the same gum for months.

Arleen blinked back to the present as the last of the clamps clanged shut on the ship. "Docking complete," the Lollapalooza's voice said into her ear-piece.

"Now what?" Arleen said into the silence.

Yosu leaned forward to scan the space their ship occupied. "I guess we wait for instructions."

Neither of them had been to this planet before. But desperate times called for desperate measures, and when the name *Fortlite372* appeared on their radar, with the mentions *fuel* and *crew for hire*, they didn't hesitate long before requesting authorization to land.

Two persons couldn't manage a ship designed for thirty for more than a few hours. One of them had to stay in the cockpit at all times, and the other had to maintain engines, check the hydraulics, dig into computing errors… It was difficult to find time to cook and eat, and impossible to fit in even twenty minutes of sleep.

They needed a crew and they needed rest. Any planet should be able to offer that. Even if none of them had ever heard of it.

"Please state your captain's name, ship's name, location of origin, and four previous destinations." The voice boomed through the docking chamber, loud enough to be heard through the glass of the cockpit's windows.

"Outside loudspeakers on," Arleen said, and watched as the corresponding button lit up on her dashboard.

"Captain Arleen Kovak," she said into the microphone. "Ship name Lollapalooza. Origin Earth." Tapping on one of her screens, she brought out a map, to make sure she got their past destinations right. She rattled them off, glancing at Yosu in case she got anything wrong.

He didn't react, only stared at the closed door some twenty yards in front of the Lollapalooza's nose, chewing at a quicker pace than usual. So either she got the ports right, or he didn't care.

"Size of crew?" the voice demanded.

"Two," Arleen replied. When there was no reply or new question, she added, "We lost most of our crew on Mansoor32. We're here to bring on new recruits."

"There is no war on Mansoor32," the voice said.

Arleen sat back in her chair, frowning. What did that have to do with anything?

Yosu pressed a button to turn on his mike. "They caught a bad case of the flu," he said. Switching his mike back off, he met Arleen's gaze. "They won't let us in if they think we're carrying a dangerous disease."

Arleen turned her own mike off, yet still whispered. "If twenty-eight persons died of this flu, I think it qualifies as dangerous."

Yosu shrugged. "If we're here, we've traveled for at least three days. If we had the flu, we'd have a fever. They can easily check that we don't."

Pursing her lips, Arleen switched her mike back on. "If you're afraid of contamination, we don't even need to get out of the docking station. Perhaps you could bring potential crew members to us?"

"You will not come in contact with anyone on Fortlite372," the voice said. Its tone remained neutral, no change from the very first question, making Arleen wonder if it was a computerized voice or if there was a person somewhere, reading instructions off a screen.

A brief pause, as loud clanks and smaller clicks sounded through the chamber. "You have been quarantined."

Arleen's head snapped around to face Yosu. His thick, dark eyebrows shot up his forehead—more expression than Arleen had seen on his face since she met him eight months ago.

He stopped chewing his gum.

※

"What does he mean, we're quarantined?" Arleen whispered. "We don't have the flu." The fatigue from the past three days was starting to catch up to her, and tears threatened to fall. She fought them back, refusing to let Yosu see any sign of weakness. She wasn't going to open herself to mutiny, even if they were quarantined.

Quarantined?

Arleen clicked through screens on her dashboard, searching for all and any information on Fortlite372. "Do you know anything about this place?" she asked her copilot. So far, all her searches turned out nothing, except for the most expensive of the star maps, which only gave a location—the only information she already had.

"No," Yosu replied, tapping on his own screen, hopefully searching for information. "I did know a Fortlite754," he offered. "It was discovered, I don't know, maybe ten years ago."

"So this planet is a young one." Arleen glued her face to the cockpit window, trying to make out as much of her surroundings as possible. But there was nothing but steel plates and bolts, with the entry closed behind them, and a smaller one—this one for people, not ships—closed in front of them.

"Or at least recently discovered," Yosu supplied. "Given the technology, I'm tempted to guess an older civilization colonized this place. If they'd been aboriginals, they wouldn't have had this level of technology. Or at least a different one."

Arleen nodded absently. Reaching a decision, she straightened in her seat. "I think we should leave. We'll figure out a way to fit some sleep into our schedule and still stay afloat, then aim for the nearest planet."

Yosu chewed his gum—slowly, as if squeezing the juice he needed out of it had to be done *just* right—before nodding. "As you wish, Captain."

Was he judging her for running away? Or did he agree with her decision? Would he have said the same if she'd proposed to send a missile at that door in front of them to see if that would get them through? Arleen just didn't know. And she couldn't ask, for fear of undermining her own authority.

She switched her mike back on. "Requesting—"

The door slid open.

A hooded creature glided through, and the door slid back closed.

"Guess we have a visitor." Not wanting to appear on the defensive, Arleen removed her harness and pressed a button to open the Lollapalooza's main door. "I'm going to meet him out there."

"Mind if I come with you, Captain?" Yosu's green eyes were calm and steady. His expression was inscrutable, completely neutral, as if he couldn't care less if Arleen accepted or refused his request.

"Please," Arleen said. "But I do the talking."

"Of course, Captain." Yosu unstrapped his harness and stood to follow.

○℥

THE HOODED FIGURE stood waiting for them on the platform. It didn't seem to be human—too tall and skinny—but it was definitely humanoid. It wore a pair of baggy trousers, in a blue material that could have passed for denim from afar, and a hooded blue sweater with a large pocket on the front. It made Arleen think of moody teenagers, but she doubted that was the effect the creature was going for.

"Greetings," she said, making a salute as she stopped a few feet in front of her host. "Captain Kovak of the Lollapalooza. We're in desperate need of a crew." When she received no response, she added, "What's this about a quarantine?"

Still no answer.

It was difficult to tell because his eyes were so small, but Arleen thought he was staring at Yosu, who was one step to the side and behind her, instead of looking at her.

Arleen gave Yosu a curt nod.

"Yosu Gaal," he said, saluting in turn. "Crew of the Lollapalooza."

"Greetings, Captain Gaal," the creature said, his voice deep, but void of any feeling. "Welcome to Fortlite372. I am Galu Palu."

Arleen pursed her lips and took a deep breath. So that's how it was, huh?

"Captain Kovak," she said in a firm voice. "I'm in charge here." She waited for Galu Palu to shift his gaze to her, but he stayed focused on Yosu.

God, she really *was* going to have a mutiny on her hands, wasn't she? She had a crew of *one*, and he managed to get the support of some alien race just by showing his face.

But Yosu kept silent. He met Galu Palu's gaze but made no move to talk. That impenetrable face of his might actually come in handy, for once.

"What's this about a quarantine?" Arleen asked. "The part of our crew who caught the flu did so over two weeks ago. If we were going to catch it, we'd be visibly sick. Most likely dead."

Still no reaction, but Arleen ignored it. "We just need to hire some crew. Minimum five or six people, just to have enough to manage the flight to an interplanetary port where we can go through a real hiring process."

In any other circumstances, Arleen would have said that two people keeping their eyes locked on each other for so long, were necessarily flirting, but Yosu and Galu Palu were like statues frozen in time.

"On the map," Arleen continued, "it said you have fuel and crew. Is this not the case? If so, please just open the hatch, and we'll be on our way. We don't have hours or days to lose by idling here."

"Captain Gaal," Galu Palu finally said in his monotone voice. "Please be informed that the quarantine has nothing to do with any disease. If your spaceship had carried any bacteria that could harm our populace, you would not have been let through our protective shield."

There had been a protective shield? Arleen hadn't even noticed. She wasn't sure if that meant their shield was very impressive, or if her inexperience as a pilot was even more so.

"It's Captain Kovak," Arleen repeated. "Then what's the quarantine for?"

The staring contest continued, Yosu staying neutral and relaxed, Galu Palu keeping his hands in the front pocket of his hoodie, tiny eyes never moving.

Galu Palu cracked after four minutes. "Captain Gaal. Please be informed that your quarantine will be lifted only when we are certain you will not be a danger to our people, and the universe in general."

Arleen barked an incredulous laugh. "Is that all? You think the two of us, and a ten-year-old spaceship—named Lollapalooza, for crying out loud—are a threat to the universe? I'm not usually one to put myself down in front of others, but I really don't think we have that sort of power." She chuckled, then sobered and added, "It's Captain Kovak."

Galu Palu didn't move a muscle. "Captain Gaal. Please be informed that we have taken it upon ourselves to protect the universe against certain dangers because nobody else is having the courage to do so. Many do not even see the danger. We do, so we act accordingly."

Placing her hands on her hips, Arleen took half a step forward to place herself in Galu Palu's line of sight. "All right, this has gone on for long enough. What's your problem, Mr. Palu? Is it beneath you to talk to women? Is that it? Do you not realize how outdated that view is? You won't be able to talk to or negotiate with over half the universe's leaders if you refuse to talk to anyone female." She waved a hand in front of Galu Palu's face. "Hello! Captain Kovak over here!"

No reaction.

The door through which Galu Palu had entered slid open. Another creature glided through, this one also wearing a hoodie—dark red and with a pocket on the front—but something much baggier on the legs. Arleen couldn't really tell if it was baggy pants or a skirt.

As the figure approached, Arleen noted that he was even taller than Galu Palu, by an inch or two.

Galu Palu bowed his head and took a step back.

"Galu Palu," the creature said. "Captain Gaal. Kovak."

The voice was as emotionless as Galu Palu's—but it was most definitely female. And she clearly had more authority than Galu Palu.

So much for the women-are-worth-less-than-men theory.

"I am Oliga Boliga," she said. "I am here to inform you that you will be in quarantine until we have proof you will not be a threat to the universe." Like Galu Palu, she addressed Yosu and completely ignored Arleen.

This was getting old. "It's Captain Kovak," Arleen said. "How exactly do you consider us to be a threat to the universe?"

This time, the silence stretched into five minutes, then ten.

Arleen risked a glance at Yosu, to judge how he felt about the proceedings. He stood at parade rest, eyes calm and meeting Oliga Boliga's, jaw working as he chewed his gum. He didn't seem to be in any hurry to speak, or do anything, really. In a way, he was even more foreign to Arleen than these tall creatures with tiny eyes, flat voices, and odd opinions on the universe.

At least he wasn't turning against her.

Oliga Boliga turned to face her compatriot, and Yosu took the opportunity to meet Arleen's eyes. He winked at her, then turned back to face their hosts—or captors, as seemed more and more likely.

Arleen and Yosu won this round, too.

"Captain Gaal," Oliga Boliga said.

"It's Captain Kovak."

"I am here to inform you that your behavior is unmitigated proof of your dangerous nature. We cannot let you leave until we have neutralized you."

That didn't sound good, no matter how you looked at it.

"And how, exactly, do you plan to go about *neutralizing* us?" Arleen asked, anger seeping into her voice.

"We will show you the path to follow," Oliga Boliga replied. "Captain Gaal," she added, just a second too late.

Arleen smiled in satisfaction. They might be pretending to address Yosu, but they were having a conversation with her.

"Not really any clearer," Arleen said, voice flat. She glanced at the large doors though which they'd entered earlier. "I'd like to request for that door to be opened, please. We're leaving."

"Captain Gaal," Oliga Boliga said. "I am here to inform you that you will not be allowed to leave until you have been neutralized."

Arleen eyed the doors again. They seemed very solid. The Lollapalooza had guns, but they weren't designed to shoot through solid steel doors, and they needed a minimum of three crew members to work them correctly. The two of them didn't stand a chance.

Only wits would get them out of this one.

"Galu Palu," Oliga Boliga said. "Please prepare the neutralization room."

Galu Palu bent his head in acknowledgment and glided to the door and out of the room.

"Captain Gaal," Oliga Boliga said. "I am here to—"

"It's Captain Kovak."

"—inform you that you and your crew must follow me. Or you will be shot." She turned her back on them and glided toward the door.

Once she was out of earshot, Yosu gave Arleen a crooked smile. "Guess we're going to the neutralization room?" He chewed at his usual pace, which calmed Arleen down. If he wasn't worried, she wouldn't be, either.

"I'd say 'after you,'" Arleen said. "But I'm the captain, so I'm going to go first."

Yosu's smile spread across his handsome face, lines appearing at the corners of his green eyes. "After you, Captain."

⁂

THE NEUTRALIZATION ROOM was all white. White walls, white floors, a white table in the middle of the room, and four white chairs. It made the people in the room, Galu Palu and Oliga Boliga, look like they were figures drawn on a white sheet of paper, not quite real and void of context.

Tiredness pulling on her eyelids and muscles alike, Arleen walked straight up to one of the chairs and sat down. Who cared if this civilization's rules said she should have waited for someone else to sit first. They were going to *neutralize* her, and she really couldn't care less about their culture and customs.

Yosu sat down next to her, pulling his chair back an inch or two, making it clear Arleen was the one in charge.

Oliga Boliga didn't care, of course. "Captain Gaal," she said in her monotone voice. "I am here to inform you that it is not acceptable for you to take orders from a little person. It is unacceptable behavior. Take control of your crew and promise not to disrupt the order of the universe in the future, and you are free to go."

Little person?

"Take it from a Tall One," Oliga Boliga continued. "We know these things. Order is to be maintained at all times, or the universe will be disturbed and we are all doomed."

Arleen's gaze moved from Oliga Boliga, to Galu Palu, and back to Oliga Boliga. Galu Palu started behaving meekly, not saying a word unless spoken to, the moment the taller woman had walked into the room.

"Are you saying your way of distributing rank is by measuring who's the tallest?" Of all the daft ideas in the world…

Oliga Boliga kept her eyes on Yosu, but she answered Arleen's question. "I am here to inform you, it is the way of the world. The Tall Ones have been given more by the gods to work with, making them stronger, faster, smarter. It is our duty to rule the universe."

Arleen let that sink in, mouth slightly ajar and hands lying flat on the table. They were serious?

"You forgot to pretend to talk to him," she said, pointing at Yosu. When she got no reaction, she added, "You didn't start or end by saying, 'Captain Gaal.' You're slipping." She flashed a smile.

Arleen thought she heard an aborted laugh from Yosu but couldn't afford to turn around to check.

"Captain Gaal," Oliga Boliga said. "Do you accept—"

"It's Captain Kovak."

"—to apply the rules put to us by the gods?"

Arleen folded her hands in her lap. She was terribly proud that her voice stayed even. "Are you suggesting that tall people are better leaders simply because they are tall? What a ridiculous notion. The size of a person's body has no impact on how his mind works."

Galu Palu spoke up for the first time since his superior's arrival. "A leader is superior to his subordinates in every way. He can run farther, reach higher, think better."

"That's where you're wrong," Arleen said. "There's no proof that a taller person can think better than a short one. There's no link between the size of a limb and the capacity of the body. And besides, what do you do when you need to get into cramped spaces?"

"Please be informed that in these cases, a real leader sends his minions to work in the cramped spaces."

"Yeah, well, I send the tall guys when I need something from the top shelf." Arleen kept her hands folded in her lap; if she let them roam free, she was afraid of the gestures they might take it upon themselves to make.

"Please be informed that working in cramped spaces is beneath a real leader."

Shaking her head, Arleen turned to Yosu. "You think they're making the rules up as we go?"

Yosu grinned, his chewing gum sticking out from his molars. "Seems possible, Captain."

Oligo Boligo stepped up to the table and took a seat. Galu Palu followed suit.

"Captain Gaal," she said. "I am here to inform you—"

"It's Captain Kovak." They were slipping in their insistence to talk only to Yosu, but Arleen had no intention of letting go.

"—that we will let you go if you accept our terms."

Yosu met Arleen's gaze, asking for permission to speak. Arleen nodded.

"I am here to inform you," Yosu started, "that I will never be the captain of the Lollapalooza."

Oligo Boligo opened her mouth to speak, but Yosu stopped her with a raised hand.

"I have been a captain in the past,"—this was news to Arleen—"and it was not the right place for me." He kept Oligo Boligo's gaze as he slowly chewed his gum. "I have had over a dozen captains since the day I boarded my first ship, and I am here to inform you that the best captains were not the tall ones. In fact, it tended to rather go in the opposite direction, since the short people have to learn authority through other means than physical intimidation.

"Captain Kovak here has only been captain for a few days, and of a rather reduced crew, but I am here to inform you that she's a much better captain than me." He leaned forward, both elbows on the white table and chewing his gum with his mouth open, making *smack, smack, smack* the only sound in the sterile room. "Am I expressing myself in a manner that you folks understand?"

Oligo Boligo's eyes seemed to draw closer to each other. Could she be frowning? "I am here to inform you that you simply need to promise to respect our rules, and we will let you go."

Yosu cocked an eyebrow. "Let me go and preach the good word to the rest of the world?" He leaned back in his chair, letting one arm drape over the backrest. "I guess I could promise that. It's just words, right? And they would get us out of here."

More chewing. "I'm guessing that's what most people do? Agree to your terms so you'll set them free?"

No reply from the captors, but Oligo Boligo was definitely frowning.

"But you're recording this, aren't you?" Yosu said. "Recording our oral contract. So once we're out there, making our way through the universe, if I ever take orders from someone shorter, or Captain Kovak gives orders to someone taller, you'll come after us, won't you? Threaten to take us to court, make sure we're unemployable. Until it's just easier to accept to live by your rules."

"And little by little," Arleen finished, "you manage to impose your world view on the universe."

It seemed ridiculous. But given enough time, and enough resources, they would be moving the universe in the direction they wanted.

Not on Arleen's watch.

"Tell you what," she said. "You claim that tall people are superior in all ways and that's why they should lead?"

Galu Palu nodded, clearly forgetting he wasn't supposed to talk to the short person.

"Well, why don't we have a demonstration?" Arleen said. "A couple of tests. If you two win against the two of us every time, you've proved your point and we'll accept your terms."

For the first time, both captors looked directly at Arleen. They considered her words for five *smacks* from Yosu before Oligo Boligo replied. "I am here to inform you that we accept your terms."

"Great!" Arleen stood up. "Where's the nearest track course?" At the blanks looks of her captors—at least that's how she interpreted them—she mimed running. "You said the tall people run faster than the short ones. Well, you can't get anyone much shorter than me—if we're talking about humans, anyway—so I'll race either one of you. Then Yosu will go up against the other one at a bout of arm wrestling."

"Sounds good to me," Yosu said, fighting a smile. If these creatures were as bad at reading their expressions as Arleen was at reading theirs, they wouldn't notice.

The two captors attempted to "inform them" of this and that for a good fifteen minutes more, but Arleen and Yosu stood their ground, throwing their own words back at them.

Finally, they went in search of a track course.

○8

THE PLANET DIDN'T have a single track course. They tried to use this as an excuse, but Arleen was on a roll, and proposed they use one of the long hallways she'd seen while walking to the white room.

Arleen stood at one end of the hallway, stretching and jumping up and down a little to get her body going. Galu Palu stood next to her, watching her every move, clearly wondering what she was up to.

Either their muscles didn't need a warm-up, or the man had never run a race in his life.

"You know," Arleen said as Yosu and two other creatures set up at the far end of the hallway. "It's not really fair that I'm the only one with something to lose in this bet." She faced Oligo Boligo, who stood ready to give the start signal. "If I win, you have to promise never to kidnap people to force your worldview on them again. On tape."

"I am here to inform you that these terms will not be accepted."

"We'll see about that," Arleen said, and crouched down, ready to sprint.

"I am here to inform you that you may start."

"Oh, for crying out—" Arleen set off, a couple of paces behind Galu Palu, who hadn't bothered to wait until the end of the sentence.

Not that it mattered.

He moved with the grace of a new-born giraffe, his legs clearly too long and weak to be able to propel him ahead at anything faster than a walking pace.

Arleen sped past him and reached the finish line in less than ten seconds.

Galu Palu limped across the line twenty seconds later, breath heaving and eyes so wide it was almost possible to see some of the whites.

"Good work, Captain," Yosu said and blew a bubble with his gum.

"You're up next." Arleen grinned at him. "There's just one thing…"

༄

It took Yosu less than a second to beat Oligo Boligo at arm wrestling. In fact, the tall creature's arm went down so fast, Arleen worried they might have broken something.

Not that it showed on her face.

"Looks like you lost again," Arleen said. "So your arguments are moot. Now, if you'll please give the word that our ship is to be allowed to leave the planet?"

Oligo Boligo did as she asked, sending one of her minions—almost as short as Arleen—to pass the word to the docking master.

"You'll also provide us with two crew members. You pick the size."

Oligo Boligo reluctantly nodded and sent off another minion. "I am here to inform you that your Yosu Gaal must let go of my hand," she said.

Indeed, Yosu still held the creature's hand against the table, and the feeble pulls Oligo Boligo's flapping arms attempted didn't stand a chance against Yosu's muscles.

"He will," Arleen said. "Once you promise to stop kidnapping people like this." She pressed a button on her intercom and a computerized voice said, "Recording."

"I am here to inform you that I will do no such thing."

Yosu moved so fast that even Arleen, who knew what was coming, was surprised. He pulled Oligo Boligo's arm around and pinned it to her back, then brought his other arm around the creature's neck in a headlock.

"We could draw this out," Arleen said. "But I'm exhausted and don't have the time or energy. So we'll make it quick. If you value your own life, you'll make the promise, or Yosu will squeeze the life out of you." She shook her head at him. "See, you're right about size mattering in some cases. But it's not about being tall, so much as being strong. And as you might notice, it's the minion, as you so charmingly call them, doing the work, and the small person making the decisions."

"Guards! T—"

Yosu tightened his hold on Oligo Boligo, effectively cutting off her air supply.

"Didn't even think to inform us?" Arleen said, affecting surprise. "Since you can't breathe, I'll be quick. Yosu will let go for ten seconds. If you don't comply, he'll tighten his grip again and not let go. This is your only chance. Understood?"

A number of creatures stood around them, shifting on their long feet, clearly uncertain of what to do. The order of things had been beat into them so soundly that if the boss didn't say to do something, they didn't do it. If they killed the boss, they might have to fight their way out, but given their general physical capacities, this didn't scare Arleen as much as it probably should.

She needn't have worried. When Yosu let go, Oligo Boligo drew a deep breath, and spewed forth her promise to never kidnap travelers and forcing her political view on them ever again.

There were probably ways around her promise, but Arleen was too tired to go into the details.

"See?" Arleen smiled. "That wasn't so hard, now was it? Captain Kovak is here to inform you that she will be leaving this planet immediately."

ॐ

"How's the new crew working out?" Arleen asked as Yosu sat down in the copilot's chair.

He shrugged. "Well enough. They must have given us what they consider to be their weakest elements, so they're both really short. Which means they don't have a problem with taking orders from me."

Arleen frowned. "But they probably won't listen to a word *I* say?"

Chuckling, Yosu leaned back to fish something out of his pocket. "Maybe you can arm-wrestle them to prove you're superior?" Paper crinkled and he popped something white into his mouth.

He offered the packet to Arleen. "Want some gum?"

AUTHOR'S NOTE

THANK YOU FOR reading *Quarantine*. I hope you enjoyed the story.

For this story, I sat down with my thesaurus and picked some random words for inspiration. I had lollapalooza (which I found to be such a fun word but kind of hard to work into the story), benevolence (or lack thereof, apparently), and quarantine. Don't know if it makes much sense but I certainly had fun writing it.

If you liked the story, you might want to check out the other stories of the Lollapalooza short story series. I have to warn you, though: the tone changes somewhat in the next ones, they're not quite as silly as this one.

I also write in a bunch of other genres. You can, for example, pick up the first book in my Tolosa Mystery series for free on my website.

R.W. Wallace
rwwallace.com

Also by R.W. Wallace

Mystery

The Tolosa Mystery Series
The Red Brick Haze (free)
The Red Brick Cellars
The Red Brick Basilica

Ghost Detective Shorts (coming soon)
Just Desserts
Lost Friends
Family Bonds
Till Death
Family History
Common Ground
Heritage
Eternal Bond
New Beginnings

Short Stories
Cold Blue Eternity
Hidden Horrors
Critters
Gertrude and the Trojan Horse
First Impressions
Let Them Eat Cake
Out of Sight
Two's Company
Like Mother Like Daughter

Fantasy (Short Stories)
Unexpected Consequences
Morbier Impossible
A Second Chance

Science Fiction (Short Stories)
The Vanguard

Lollapalooza Shorts
Quarantine
Common Enemies
Coiled Danger
Mars Meeting

Adventure (Short Stories)
Size Matters

www.ingramcontent.com/pod-product-compliance
Lightning Source LLC
LaVergne TN
LVHW041717060526
838201LV00043B/785